Vincent Paints His House

TEDD ARNOLD

Holiday House / New York

For Jeanie and Henri

HOLIDAY HOUSE is registered in the U.S. Patent and Trademark Office.
Printed and Bound in April 2015 at Tien Wah Press, Johor Bahru, Johor, Malaysia.
The artwork was rendered digitally using Photoshop software.
www.holidayhouse.com
First Edition
1 3 5 7 9 10 8 6 4 2

Library of Congress Cataloging-in-Publication Data
Arnold, Tedd, author, illustrator.
Vincent paints his house / by Tedd Arnold. — First edition.
Summary: Vincent's animal friends disagree on how he should
paint his house, so Vincent comes up with a colorful solution.
ISBN 978-0-8234-3210-3 (hardcover)
[1. House painting—Fiction. 2. Color—Fiction. 3. Animals—Fiction.] I. Title.
PZ7.A7379Vi 2015
[E]—dc23
2014006045

"Hmm . . . ,"
said Vincent.

Vincent could not decide what color to use.

"Maybe
I will just
paint it white,"
said Vincent.

"White is nice," said Vincent.

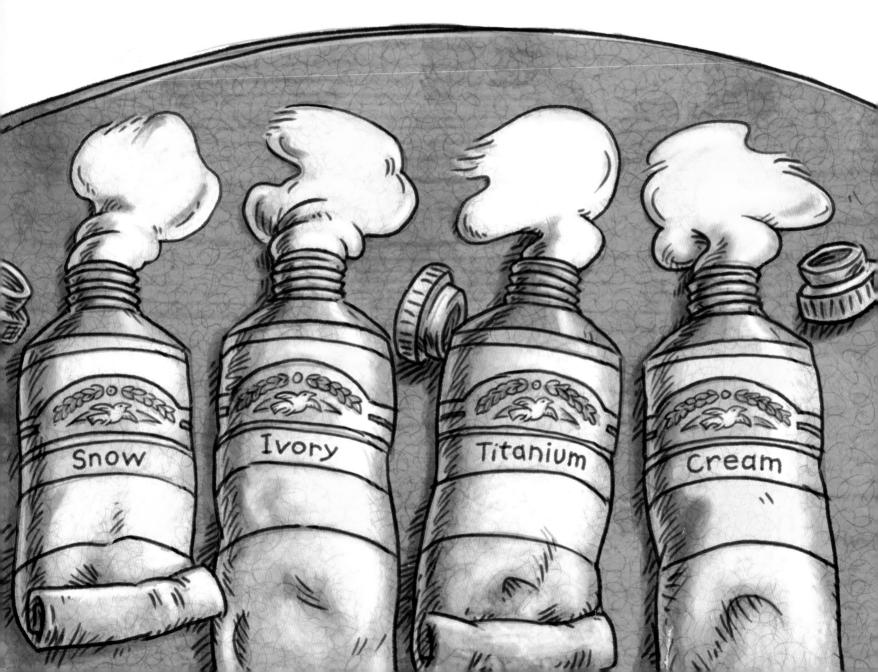

"Stop!" said the spider. "This is MY house, and I like red."

"Red is nice," said Vincent.

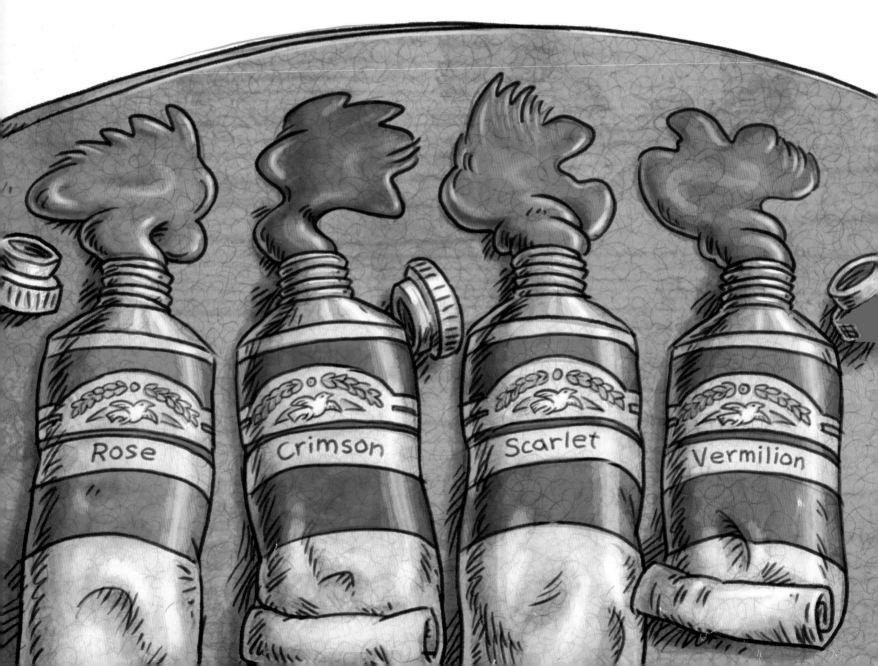

"Stop!" said the caterpillar. "This is MY house, and I like yellow."

"Yellow is nice," said Vincent.

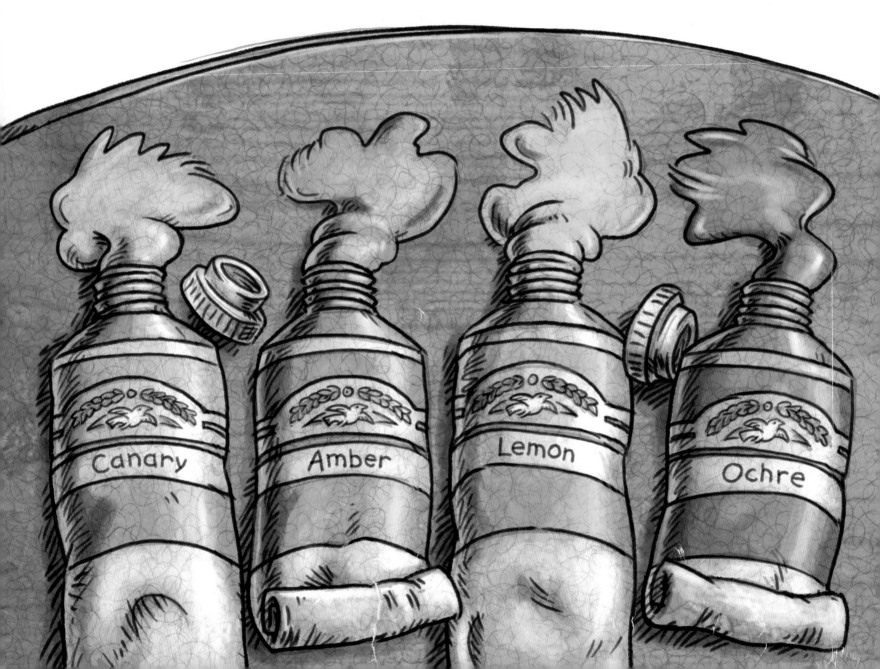

"Stop!" said the beetle. "This is MY house, and I like purple."

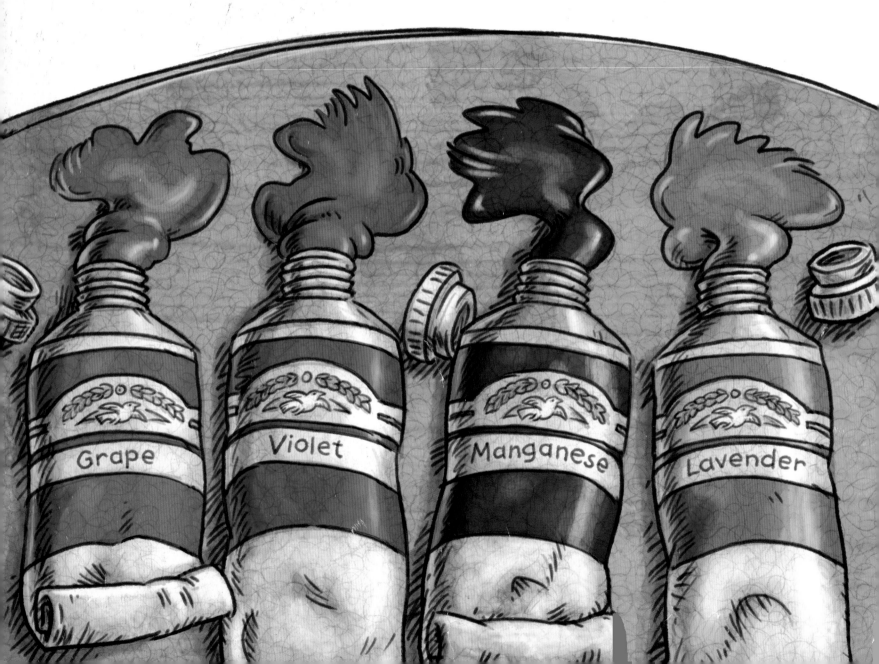

"Purple is nice," said Vincent.

"Stop!" said the bird. "This is MY house, and I like blue."

"Blue is nice," said Vincent.

"Orange is nice," said Vincent.

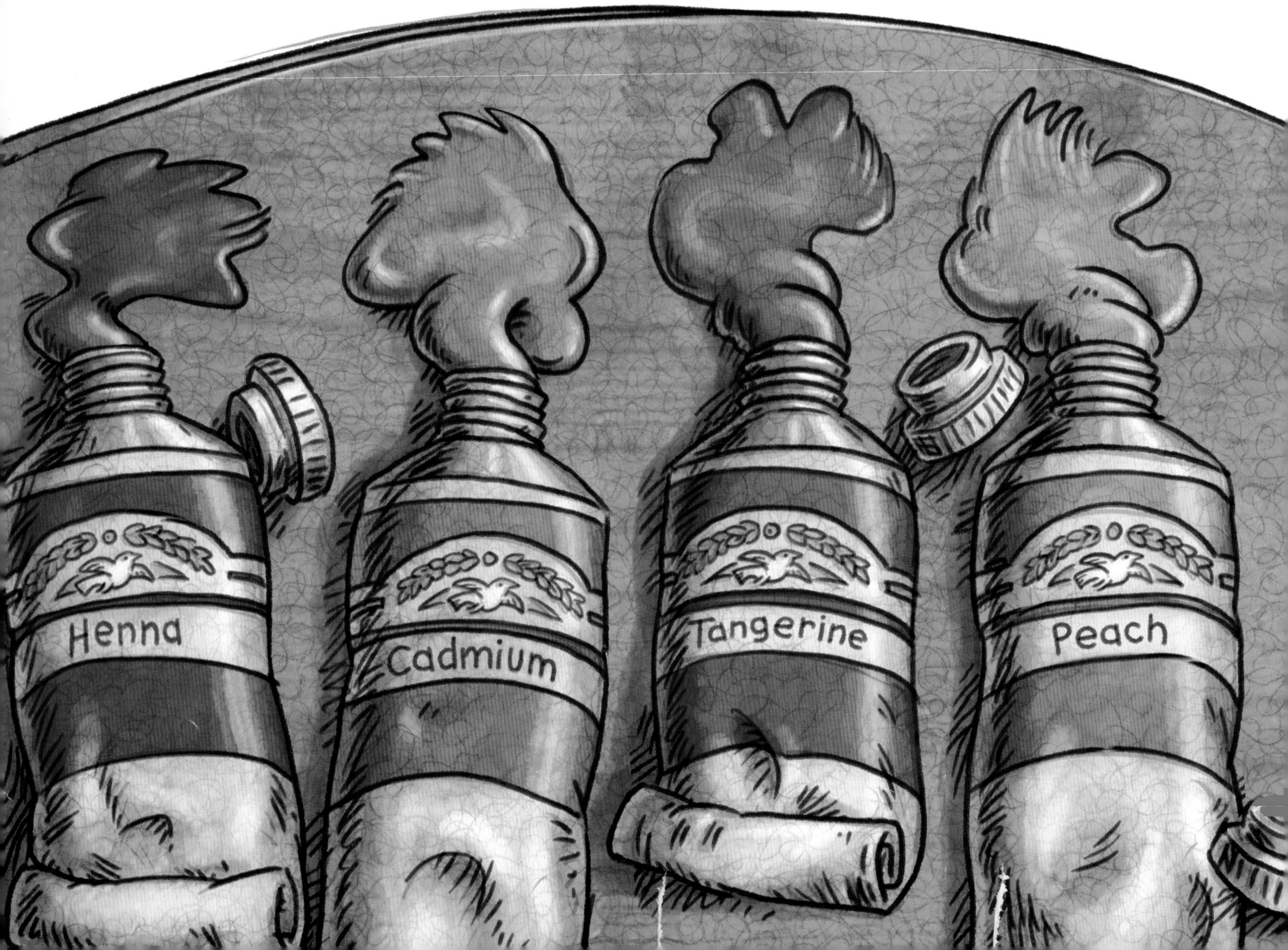

Henna

Cadmium

Tangerine

Peach

"Stop!" said the snake.
"This is MY house, and
I like green."

"Green is nice," said Vincent.

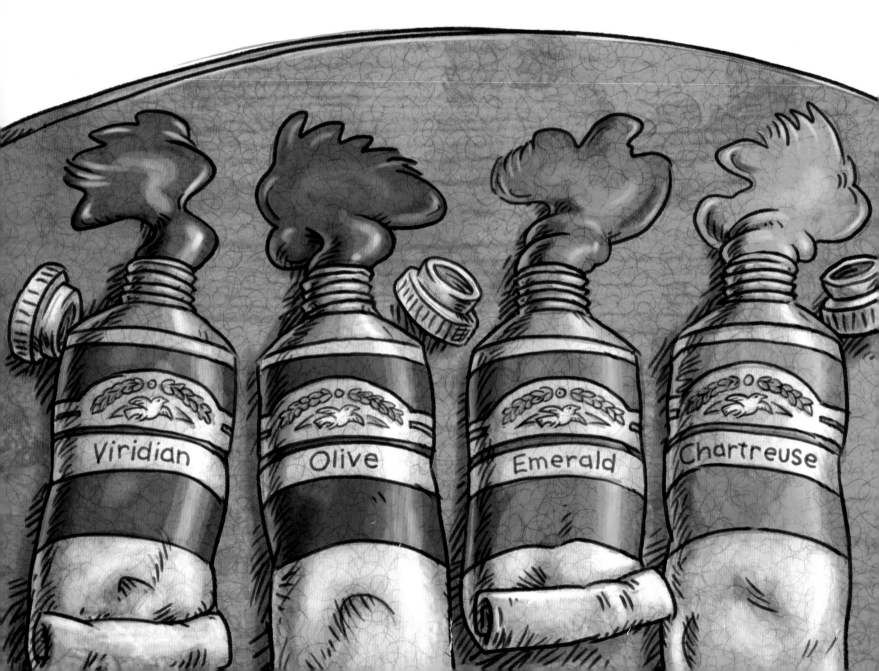

"Stop!" said the mouse. "This is MY house, and I like brown."

"Stop!" said the bat. "This is MY house, and I like black."

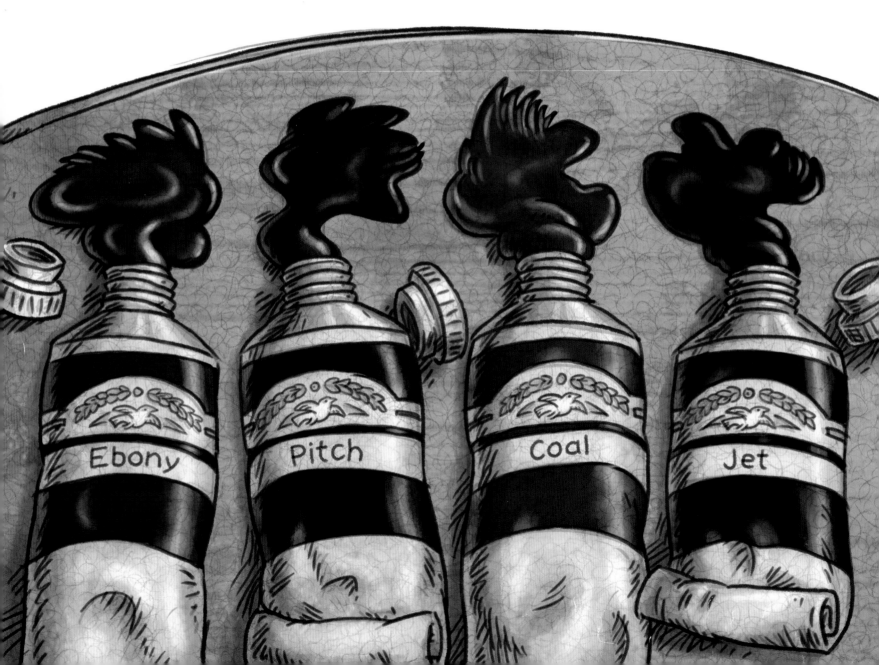

"Black is nice," said Vincent,

"but actually, this is my house!"

Everyone was happy!

The End